GOODBYE, MY ISLAND

JEAN ROGERS

GOODBYE, MY ISLAND

Illustrated by RIE MUÑOZ

GREENWILLOW BOOKS
New York

Library of Congress Cataloging in Publication Data
Rogers, Jean.   Goodbye, my island.
Summary: Twelve-year-old Esther Atoolik
tells of the last winter her people spent on
King Island, Alaska, in the early 1960s.
[1. Eskimos—Fiction.   2. Alaska—Fiction]
I. Muñoz, Rie, ill.   II. Title
PZ7.R6355Go 1983   [Fic]   82-15816
ISBN 0-688-01964-1
ISBN 0-688-01965-X (lib. bdg.)

FOR
GOOD, KIND,
ENCOURAGING
HUSBAND,
FRIENDS,
AND ESPECIALLY RIE
FOR HER INSPIRATION

GLOSSARY

Auklet (crested auklet) a small bird with a tuft of feathers and a distinctive orange spot on its head. Other birds commonly found on King Island would be puffins, murres, snow buntings, sea gulls, and jaegers.

Bearded seal largest of the seals in the waters around King Island. It is much prized for meat and skin.

Beluga a small, white whale found in northern waters

Eskultea an Eskimo word for school teacher

Gussuk Eskimo slang used to designate a white person. It is believed to derive from the Russian cossack.

Leads openings or cracks between cakes or floes of ice

Mukluk a sealskin boot worn by Eskimos

Muktuk skin of whale with blubber (fat), much prized as food

Oomiak a large, open boat made of walrus skin stretched over a wooden frame. Seams are sewn by the women and overlapped in such a way as to be completely watertight. King Island oomiaks were often as large as thirty feet long.

GOODBYE,
MY ISLAND

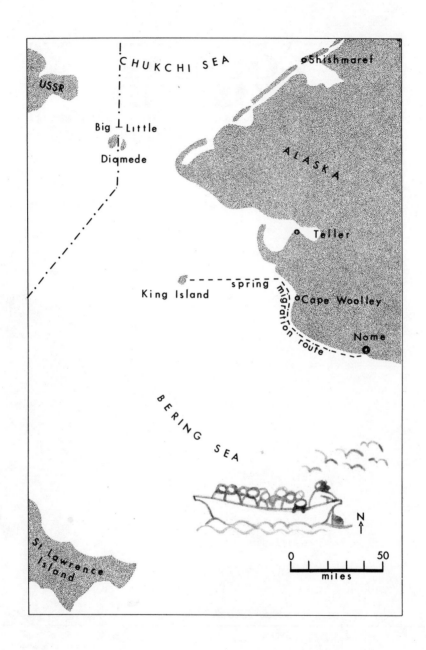

ONE

Today I, Esther Atoolik, am the happiest girl in Nome, Alaska. Today we are going home to King Island. Today is also my twelfth birthday, but the happiness that is growing and growing inside me is all because we are going home, we King Islanders.

All summer we live in Nome. We come in our biggest skin boats, our oomiaks, on the last day of June. The oomiaks are loaded with our gear and the ivory pieces that were carved during the long winter when the ice holds us fast on our island. During the summer our men work in Nome or carve more ivory to sell to the tourists. We come here to Nome and camp on the beach with the others, the people from Little Diomede, from Shishmaref, from St. Lawrence Island. We all come to Nome for the summer. We islanders have always done this.

Our oomiaks will not carry everything we have bought in Nome. We have bought so many, many things to take home. Today the big boat, the *North Star*, is going south for the very last time until next spring. She will stop and let us off on King Island. The men and boys are busy loading her. Right now they are loading the oomiaks with the big oil drums, enough to keep us warm all winter in the school-house and in the church. Our tents and our pots and our groceries and our tea and the berries we picked in Nome have already been taken to the boat. Silook and Ooloranna are watching everything to see that nothing is left behind. Nothing must be forgotten, not a single thing, because soon the long dark and the big ice will come, and we will be frozen fast on our island for the rest of the winter. When the ice melts, we will return to Nome. So it is.

Mary and I and Mary's *gussuk* friend Vicky are watching the oomiaks hurry out to the *North Star* and unload, then hurry back to the beach to be loaded again. Last of all, the people will climb into the boats, putt-putt-putt out to the big boat, climb onto the hoist, and be lifted up to the deck. Even our oomiaks get a ride on that hoist. Oh, how that strange ride used to frighten me. The hoist swung and swayed and swooped, and there was only my mother's hand to keep me from the greedy mouths of the waves. They looked so big, those waves, ready to swallow me up in one gulp. Now I am like my brother, Lewis. We like the ride. We like to swing out above the big, hungry waves. It makes us laugh. And I know it means we will soon be home again.

Now comes the only sadness of this day. Mary and I must say goodbye again.

I was so happy to see Mary when our oomiaks pulled up onto the beach last spring. I knew Mary would be there, and she was. First I had to tell her about everything that had happened on King Island. Had anyone died or been born? Whether the seal and walrus hunts and the egg gathering had been good or bad, how Father Tomas had celebrated Christmas, and was it the same as always? She wanted to know everything before she would let me ask a single question about her first winter in Nome.

We talked and talked all the while we were helping unload the boats and set up our camp in the old army Quonset huts left over from World War II.

"You two sound like a whole flock of birds," my brother said, laughing at us. "Sea gulls." We did not mind his teasing that day.

When Mary's family did not come back to King Island last fall, it made me very sad. There is no longer another girl my age in the village. My mother has been worrying for a long time because so many King Islanders have stayed in Nome. But I did not notice it until Mary's house stood empty all winter long. Then I looked around me and saw that many other houses were also empty, and I began to listen to the talk. How soon would the Bureau of Indian Affairs close the school? What would we do then? How long would Father Tomas keep coming when so many families did not return? What would happen to the King Islanders who did not ever want to leave? Would there be too few to stay? Would they be allowed to stay if there were no school for their children? What was going to happen to the co-op store? Everyone knew it was not going well. My ears heard all these questions, but my ears did not hear any answers. It was a worry.

"I like the school here the best," Mary told me, after she had heard all about our winter on the island. "I have a *gussuk* friend in school. Her name is Vicky, and she talks all the time. The questions she asks! She is so funny. I told her about you. She says she is dying to meet you. Her father is the principal of the school. They have gone away for the summer, but they will be back. You will meet her, and you will know what I mean. She wants to be your friend, too."

"What is so good about school in Nome?" I asked Mary.

"Oh, there are so many things it will take a long time to tell you. My mother has a job at school every day helping cook lunch. We get a hot lunch every day, not just some soup or a hot drink like on King Island. At first I didn't like the lunch, but then my mother came to help cook, and now I like it a lot. There are so many things to do, too. We have movies all the time."

"In school?" I asked. "Right in school?"

"Oh, yes," Mary said. "Not like the ones we saw downtown last summer, but others. Lots of others. There are things to play with out on the playground. We can go there and play anytime we like even when there is no school. There's a slide and swings and a big climbing thing that is fun if the big boys are not on it. I will show you, and we can play there."

It was a long time before Mary mentioned any but the good things about Nome. "I did miss you so much," she said. "I wish you were going to stay. There is one bad thing. The people from Shishmaref and St. Lawrence Island do not like us. They say they came here first and we just followed them. The big boys and sometimes the big girls fight about it. Vicky says it is just silly; we are all Eskimos, and where we come from doesn't matter. We should all be friends now that we are here. That's what Vicky says. Vicky always takes my side when the girls from Shishmaref tease me on the playground, but sometimes I wish I were safe at home on King Island. Some days it was so bad at school, and I needed you more than ever.

"The teacher does not allow any teasing in the school, not in our room anyway. There are lots of rooms in the school here, and only boys and girls of the same age are in the room with you.

"My big brothers, Anok and Anuya, say it is not so in their room. The other big boys say that we

King Islanders are not as good as they are, and they don't want to have anything to do with anyone from our village. Anok says that all their teacher says when the boys fight is that they must learn to get along, but he does not stop the taunting, and the boys from King Island get blamed for fighting. Anok had two black eyes, and Anuya had to go to the hospital because he needed stitches in his cheek. He said he fell on the ice, but at school we all knew his face got cut in a fight with a boy from St. Lawrence Island.

"But now I will tell you only pleasant things. Do you know, Esther, all winter long you can go to the grocery store and buy apples and oranges and anything you want? Candy, too. Well, anytime you have the money. There are a lot of places you need money in Nome."

Those first days in Nome this summer had my head in a whirl. Mary had so much to tell me and so many things to show me. I had spent many summers in Nome, but Mary says all the best things in Nome happen in winter.

"Don't you miss King Island and being home?" I asked her.

"Yes, I do, and I especially miss you and all the things we used to do together. Here I belong to a Girl Scout troop that meets every week after school. We make popcorn and candy and learn songs. Vicky says maybe we can go to a camp sometime. You could come too, Esther." I did not tell Mary about the worrying talk I had heard all last winter. I did not want to talk about it. I do not want to think about not going back home.

"The Shishmaref kids say that King Island is just a big empty rock and that only crazy people would ever live there. They say we are really crazy birds who just think they are people. Doesn't that make you laugh?"

Even on this last day Mary was still telling me about the many things there are to do in Nome all winter long. "There are airplanes coming in every day if it isn't too stormy, and even *gussuk* tourists who come and ride on the dogsleds and watch the fishing out on the ice. They buy ivory things all winter long, and my father has no trouble selling his work to the stores. He is one of the best carvers here in Nome. He always gets a good price for his ivory," Mary boasted, and I knew it was true. "And he always brings the money home and never stops to drink at the bar. Not like Wooko."

I knew about Wooko. He and his wife, Vivian, had stayed in Nome last winter, but this winter they were going back to King Island with us. Vivian said she would not stay another winter in Nome. All Wooko wanted to do was to get drunk and stay drunk. He forgot that he had two little girls to feed and a wife who needed a fire to cook on. He forgot everything except getting to the bar when it opened in the morning and staying there until he was thrown out at night. Vivian said she was tired of going to get him and helping him stagger home so he wouldn't freeze on the street. She talked about it so much that Wooko gave her a black eye and a split lip and she had to go to her neighbors and ask them to take her in with her little girls.

When Ooloranna came, Vivian and Wooko talked to him, and he said Wooko should come back with us to where there was no bar and where Wooko could carve in peace all winter long. Wooko gave his summer earnings to Ooloranna as soon as he was paid, and just before we left, Ooloranna gave him the money so he could buy all the things his family would need for the long winter.

Lewis came running up to us—Mary, Vicky, and me—as we stood talking and watching.

"Teachers are here, teachers are here," he shouted happily. "And guess what, you'll never guess what."

"Well, what?" asked Vicky.

"Marie and Roger have a big boy with them. This year he is going to be their boy. He is just my age! I have already seen him, and they have asked me to be his friend." Lewis's smile was so big his face disappeared behind it.

"How did they manage to get a boy just your age?" Mary wanted to know.

"He is the son of teacher's sister. Marie said he is her nephew. He is going to spend the year on King Island, and I will teach him all about it and how to hunt and fish and make a sled for the ice and everything."

The *North Star* blew its loud whistle. It was time for us to go.

"Oh, I wish you were staying with Vicky and me," Mary moaned. She had been saying that all day. "We could have so much fun if you could stay. Winter is the best, best time in Nome." I kept my face down so Mary couldn't see the happiness in my eyes. I wasn't happy to be leaving her, but I was, oh, so happy to be going home. My heart was singing as I climbed into the oomiak with my family. We waved to our friends lined up on the beach. I was so happy I did not notice how many people remained on the shore. I did not think of the empty houses there would be on King Island this winter. I thought only that at last we were going home.

TWO

Yakuk was the first person to see our island. He is one of the best hunters because his eyes are so keen. He is always the one to see the first polar bear on the ice. "See that thin white line," he said. "That is King Island." Soon we all could see it, our big rock, sitting alone out there in the sea. Soon we could see specks, sea gulls wheeling in the sky above it, and then the waves splashing on the big rocks. King Island comes straight up out of the sea, up, up, more than a thousand feet, teacher says. Our little village clings to the side of the rock. It looks so small I think maybe the Shishmaref boys are right, that our people are descended from the bird spirits and long ago built our houses, like strange square nests, in the little nooks and crannies of this steep rock.

But now we have to hurry, hurry. The *North Star* is eager to go south, and we must get all our things off as fast as we can. Everyone knows just what to do. We have done this every year for as long as anyone can remember.

First the oomiaks are lowered, and down we go in the hoist, one last wild ride. Everything must be taken to shore in our boats and stacked on the big boulders, safe from the splashing water, until we can carry it up to the houses. All the men know just exactly how much they can carry each trip. What a bustle. Everyone is happy to be back. Birds are squawking and crying above us. The dogs we left in June are down on the rocks, barking to welcome us and fighting for places on the big rocks nearest the water. There is laughing and shouting and noise from the motors. There are our two dogs. Lewis and I spot them together. Good. They have managed to catch enough birds and eggs to survive during the months we were gone.

Mother and Lewis and I have a long climb to our

house. We carry our loads, first up the path and then to the wooden steps. Father is making more trips in the oomiak, as fast as he can. So many things to unload for all of us and the teachers' and Father Tomas's things as well. Stuff is piling up on our rocky shore in big heaps. It will take us three days to get everything hauled up to the village. Father Tomas will go straight to the church and direct the storing away of his things. Marie will do the same at the school: school supplies in the schoolroom and food and fuel in the storage shed at the back. The oil drums will be the very last because it doesn't matter if they get wet. Besides, it takes all the men to pull them up to the schoolhouse and the church.

What a happy time this is in our King Island village. We are all working together so that we will be safe and comfortable in the coming winter. When the unloading is done, Father Tomas will hold a service in the church and the teachers will give a party at the schoolhouse.

THREE

Lewis brought Dixon to see where we live. Dixon is the teachers' nephew. He is the same age as Lewis, but he is much broader and taller. He talks as much and asks as many questions as Mary's friend Vicky. His speech sounded full of funny sputters because he talked so fast and kept saying, "What's this? What's that?"

"Uncle Roger says you and Lewis speak the most English," he said to me. "So I can ask you everything I want to know. It is so different here I want to know everything." We all laughed, Mother, too. She does not speak English much, but she understands. In our house it is our father who speaks English. He spent many years in the hospital when he was a boy. He was flown from Nome to the Alaska Native Hospital in Anchorage, where the doctors kept him until he was a young man. But he never forgot his home on King Island, and he has never gone away again. The other men who speak English learned it in the army or in the hospital like Father. Some of the women, too, have learned English, especially

Etta, who works at the school and translates for the children what the teachers are saying. Lewis and I do that, too. We learned English from Father. He told Mother that in these days to speak Eskimo is not enough. He says that often. Mother can speak English, too, when she wants to, but she is shy and does not like to do it when others are present.

Dixon is nice, and I did not mind that he asked us about everything.

"Why is your door only sort of a window?" he asked as he stepped into our house. "Why does it open only at the top half?" True, our doors are not like the doors in the schoolhouse or church. Our doors start halfway up the house wall, and there is only one door, not like at school.

"To keep out the cold," Lewis explained. "It gets very, very cold in the winter." I could tell by the look on Dixon's face that he didn't understand.

"See," I said. "We have no chairs. We sit on the floor in our houses. If our doors opened all the way down, the cold would creep in under the door."

"Sure," said Dixon. "I see." Mother was lighting the Coleman stove to make tea. Lewis offered some to Dixon. "Is that your only stove?" he asked. "Do you do all your cooking on that?"

Lewis nodded, passing the sugar to Dixon. "We are lucky to have a stove like this," he said. "We used to cook over a seal-oil lamp. Now most of us on King Island have Coleman stoves. The lamp gives us light and keeps us warm."

"Where are your beds?" asked Dixon. He looked all around the small room that is our house with his eager, searching eyes, asking and asking. Ours was the very first house he had been in on King Island. Lewis showed him our furs and blankets on the racks along one wall, our tea and sugar and kettles in the boxes, our pee pot over beside the door, our water can with its dipper, our clothes hanging on their pegs, everything.

Dixon turned to me. "Can I ask you a question?" We all laughed at that. Even my mother, who is so polite, laughed behind her hand. What had Dixon been doing but asking questions so fast that Lewis barely had time to answer? Dixon laughed, too, as I nodded. "All you girls are wearing print dresses. I thought Eskimos wear fur parkas like Marie and Roger do."

"We do, but they are kept for special occasions, Dixon. See, this is our father's hanging here." Lewis took Father's fur parka from its hook and showed

Dixon the fur strips that made the design, the wolf fur that trimmed the parka hood. "These take a lot of time to sew," Lewis explained. "Special fur has to be collected to make the pattern come out just right. If you have a parka as fine as this one, you don't go hunting or fishing in it; for that, you wear your everyday parka with the skin side out. Show him, Esther."

I put on my reindeer skin parka and put my blue parka cover over it, the one Mother made new for me just before we went to Nome. She would make me another one soon of the calico we had ordered from the catalog while we were there. The skin was tanned so that it was soft and white; the fur side turned in kept me warm as warm. Lewis showed Dixon Father's white parka cover that he wore hunting. We girls and women never go hunting, so our parka covers can be the brightest colors and patterns that we can find.

I knew why Dixon wanted to know about everything because that is the way we are when we go to the schoolhouse. We want to see and touch everything that is so different—the glass windows that look out over the sea, the stove in teacher's room that is big and black and so hot all the time. It has an oven where Teacher Marie can make bread and cookies; she has let me help her do this. At our house we have pilot bread from the store to dip in our stew or our tea.

"When the shore ice freezes hard enough," Lewis told Dixon, "I will take you to the big ice cave where we store our meat all winter long. Big Peter says the cave is so long it goes all the way through our island and comes out on the other side."

"Wow, really?" Dixon said. "Really?"

"Well, I've never been all the way through it, but that's what Peter says," Lewis said. He was proud to be the one to tell Dixon about our King Island.

FOUR

After the church service there was the party at the school. Everybody crowded into the schoolroom. By the door there was just one big pile of parkas and jackets. Roger and Marie had pushed the desks along the wall to make a table for the food.

All the women brought something good to eat. Father went in his kayak to the ice cave where our meat is kept to get some whale meat. Then Mother made beluga stew. How delicious it smelled when it was cooking. I could not wait to taste it. Beluga stew is my favorite dish, almost.

Sure enough, Marie had made loaves and loaves of bread and a big mound of cookies. Peter brought a big can of Crisco from the store to spread on the bread. We could spread it as thick as we liked. There were so many good things to eat it was as good as Christmas or Easter. We were so happy to be home again.

After the eating was over came the speeches. First Ooloranna, of course. "Father." He nodded to Father Tomas. *"Eskultea,"* he said to the teachers. At school the teachers do not want us to call them *eskultea*—they want us to call them Roger and Marie—but they smile when Ooloranna says *eskultea*. He always says a few words in English and then some words in Eskimo for the elders who do not follow English well. Then he smiles and asks Father Tomas if he wants to say anything. Father Tomas says he has already had his turn at the church, but he must just say another thank-you for all the fine food he has eaten and because we are together again and he has been granted the privilege of being with us for another year. Everyone laughs with Father Tomas. Every year he says he has nothing more to say and then adds these same words. Now Peter says he must say a few words about the store. He is not smiling.

"You know how long it was," he said, "before we could make the Bureau of Indian Affairs let us have a co-op store here on King Island. Only a few years ago, to help us through the winters, were we able to open our store. Now they tell me our store must close after this winter. We cannot buy groceries for next year because we still owe for things we bought last winter and the winters before that. That is the way it is." Peter sat down. There was whispering and nodding as those who spoke English explained to the others what had been said.

"It is true." Ooloranna nodded.

The schoolteacher rose. "I, too, have bad news," Roger said. He spoke slowly, with long pauses, so everyone could hear and understand. "The Bureau of Indian Affairs has told me, too, that this is the last year there will be a school on King Island. I am very sorry to say this as Marie and I have enjoyed our teaching here very much. But the education department says it is costing too much per pupil to maintain a school here, and the last ten years have shown a steady decline in the numbers. In 1950 there were forty-nine students attending the King Island school and pupils came for half days only, older ones in the morning and younger ones in the afternoon. Now everyone comes both sessions, but last year there were only seventeen pupils. Probably there will be even fewer this year. Let's see, how many of you will be coming to the school this year?" Even with Dixon, I could count only twelve. I would be the oldest girl in the school. Tillie did not put up her hand; even last year she had thought she was too old for school, and Annie, the other biggest girl, had stayed in Nome.

"You see how it is," said Roger sadly.

Inside me a bad feeling twisted and turned like a bird trying to free itself from the net. How many times our father had told us that it was important that we attend the white man's school and learn all we could. "The old Eskimo ways are slowly leaving us," he said. "It is up to you who are young to learn all you can about the new ways. You will have to learn the new ways to survive." I wondered now if Lewis and I had learned enough. With no school what would become of us? How would the smaller ones learn enough? I did not want to admit to myself what it would mean to King Island if there were no school and no co-op store.

I tried as hard as I could to push away these thoughts and enjoy the rest of the party. Ooloranna got out his drum, and so did Adsun. The oldest women put on their white gloves to begin the dance. I heard Lewis telling Dixon what they were doing.

"I don't know why they wear white gloves for dancing," he said, "only that they always do." How I wish that nothing would ever change on our King Island, that we could go on as we always have.

FIVE

School began the next day. Lewis and I climbed up the few stairs from our house to the porch built in front of the schoolhouse, even before the bell rang. Dixon was there waiting to pull the rope that rang the bell. He said Lewis could help him. I went on in to see if I could help Etta and Marie. If Mary had been there, we would have stayed on the porch to talk awhile and watch all the others come. Or maybe we would have played ball. The ball bounces well on the porch of the schoolhouse, and we never let it get away from us, well, not often anyway.

"Oh, good," Marie said when she saw me. "You can lend us a hand here, Esther. Etta and I are getting a corner ready for the littles." Roger came out of the storeroom with two of the smallest desks for them.

"We'll have two new pupils this year," Marie said. "Wooko and Vivian's older girl, Rose, is coming to school, and Peter, George's smallest boy. How nice that we will have a new boy and girl."

There was a surprise for us when the bell rang. Tillie came in with the others. "I decided to come after all," she said. "If this is going to be the last year, I thought maybe I had better learn all I can." She laughed. I was glad she had come. Now I would not be alone with the big boys, Nat and Paul. On the days when they went hunting, I would have someone to share lessons with, and knitting and sewing.

First we talked about what we had done in Nome all summer. Then Roger and Marie told us about their visits home in the state of Wisconsin. "We went to school, too, for six weeks," Roger told us. That made us laugh. Roger and Marie knew so much how could they learn anything more? "Then we visited our families. We had a good time this summer, but we're glad to be back," Roger said.

Then Dixon told us about himself. "I'm eleven years old," he said. "This is the first time I have ever been out of the state of Wisconsin, and I sure have come a long way. I'm used to cold weather and ice and snow, but Uncle Roger tells me I have never seen a winter like the winters you have on King Island. I am looking forward to being frozen in and having night all day long and sliding down your steep slopes and learning to catch fish and crab through the ice and going hunting and everything." That Dixon was some talker. He wasn't shy like I was when I first came to school. Even now it is so hard for me to stand up and speak in front of everyone. It is hard to find the right words.

Marie said anyone who wanted to could stay awhile after school and start our knitting projects. "We'll get a good early start," she said. "You can get lots of mittens and socks done for Christmas presents. Everything can have a nice red trim this year. I've brought a big box of red yarn." Many of us stayed, both boys and girls. We all like to knit. Marie made tea for us. While we were drinking it, Marie said to me, "Esther, I'm going to give you a special job this year. Every week you can write in the school log for us about the most important things that have happened on King Island during that week. You can be our reporter, Esther. We want to make this last year as important as we can in every way."

"Oh." I gasped. "I don't write well, I couldn't . . ."

"Oh, yes, you can." Marie smiled at me. "You're one of our best writers, and I'll help you anyway. You can write it out on a piece of scratch paper first, and I will help you correct it. Then you can copy it in the logbook. You can do it, Esther. We'll do it every Friday afternoon."

I was scared, but I was proud. My words, my very own writing to go in the big logbook. At first I thought it would be very hard to know what to put down, but when Friday came, there seemed to be so much to write about that I would not be able to tell it all. Here is what I wrote:

We all are happy to be back on our island. When we finished unloading, Father Tomas held a service and the teachers gave a party. We have a new boy in our school this year, Dixon. Tillie came back, too. There are thirteen pupils. Rose and Peter are the smallest, and Nat and Paul are the big ones. Dixon likes it here very much.

Marie spelled some words for me, and I copied them in the log. Roger said it was a good idea, and he was glad I was doing it. He wrote at the end: "by Esther Atoolik, King Island, September 27, 1963."

FRIDAY, OCTOBER 4

Storms come every day now. There is much snow but it is not too cold except in the wind. No hunting, and the ice is not strong enough yet for fishing.

OCTOBER 11

The weather has been bad and much knitting has been done. One day we showed Dixon the string games. Silook came that day to show new string games to us. He knows many, most of anybody.

OCTOBER 18

The whole school went out to watch the stopping of the biggest dogfight. All the men came running, and the boys helped, too, to pull the dogs apart. Dogs fight very often, but this was one big fight. It was the biggest happening of this week at our school on our island.

OCTOBER 25

No school for three days. A big rainstorm washed away all the snow. Big rocks slid down and hit the school at one end. Teacher Roger and Adsun and Charlie had a job making the corner stand up again, so that no water came in. Lucky no windows were broken, Adsun said.

NOVEMBER 1

Dixon and Teacher Marie gave a Halloween party in school. Just like in Wisconsin, Dixon said. They showed us how to make masks of orange paper, big jack-o'-lantern faces to hide behind. Cookies for all. We laughed a lot.

SIX

The ice was very late coming this year. Father says that some years are like that. All years are different. Dixon was very anxious for it to freeze for two reasons: He wanted to try fishing through the ice, and he wanted to try out the sleds, which are made from one ski. We can't slide on our sleds until the shore ice has hardened so we won't fall into the water and drown. Ice packs were drifting all around us, but the shore ice, the ring of ice that fastens itself to our rock and gets thicker until it is safe to walk on, was not yet hard enough.

"It will come," Lewis promised Dixon. "Don't worry. It has always come, and this year it will come, too. We can go to the clubhouse and watch Wooko and Pica carve their ivory. Marta and Lily are scraping a walrus hide there, too." I went with the boys. Mother was at Vivian's, having a talk and tea. No one was playing outside because of the freezing rain. I wished for Mary. Mary and I could always find something to do. Perhaps Lily would be at the clubhouse.

Dixon and Lewis and I climbed under the club-house and wriggled up through the hole that led inside. Dixon was laughing all the time. He thought our window-doors were funny, but he thought the door to the clubhouse was the funniest of all. First we crawl through a tunnel that comes out in the very center of the clubhouse floor. Then we push ourselves up through the hole into the clubhouse. That way the cold and wind are fooled and do not come in with us. Lily was not there, but I decided to stay awhile. Then I went home to help Mother with our supper. Later, when Lewis came back, he was covered with snow. That was the last we saw of any rain.

NOVEMBER 15

Chuna cut his leg on a piece of ice, playing on his sled. Teacher Roger said the cut needed stitches, so Paul ran for Mrs. Tooliak, and she sewed him up. Roger made him a big bandage. This happened this week at school.

NOVEMBER 22

Teachers told us about Pilgrims and Thanksgiving. Dixon told us turkey is the best bird to eat. We told

31▼▼

him here the best food is beluga stew. Just then Father
Tomas came to tell us the sad news he heard on his
radio. Our U.S. President Kennedy has been shot
dead. Soon our whole village came to talk about this
big news. Father Tomas said a prayer, and we felt sad
for this bad happening. Marie made tea for everyone,
and there was no more school this day.

NOVEMBER 29

Big storm all week. Very strong wind, blowing snow.
Much cold, dark. Dixon stood up in school and said
how he liked coming to school in the dark and going
home when it was already dark. He told about riding
to school in Wisconsin in a big yellow bus. The
teachers showed us pictures of the bus and school.
Dixon said he liked climbing up and down the wooden
stairs in our village better than the bus.

SEVEN

The shore ice was fast and firm, so Lewis and I and Mother showed Dixon how to chop a hole in it with a chisel. Then Mother scooped out the ice pieces. Dixon lowered his line while Mother and I chopped another hole nearby. There were many holes being readied for fishing. Besides me and my mother and Lewis, there were Vivian and Marta and Etta and Ooloranna's wife, Ruth. She loves to fish and fishes even on the coldest days. She laughs when people tell her it is too cold for an old woman to stand out on the ice and jiggle a fish line in the water. "Not too cold for fish to bite, not too cold for me," she says. When thin ice forms over the hole, Mother scoops it out. Otherwise, the fish would be knocked off the hook. That was what happened to Dixon's first fish. He didn't understand why it happened.

"Here, see how my mother does it," Lewis said, bringing Dixon over to watch. Carefully, oh, so slowly, Mother was bringing up her line. A fine small bullhead was on the hook. Carefully, carefully

Mother drew the fish through the hole in the ice and shook it off the hook.

"Oh, I see," Dixon cried. "We're using barbless hooks. How come, Lewis, how come?"

"It's too cold to take off your mittens and handle a wet fish. Your fingers would turn to ice right away. You have to be able to get the fish off the hook and keep your mittens safely on."

"Yeah, I do see. That's pretty smart, Lewis. Who thought of that?"

"It has always been so," Lewis answered.

When Mother brought up a crab, we gathered around and enjoyed a taste of fresh crab. First we let it freeze a little bit; then we ate it. Dixon was very excited. He said he had never seen anyone eat crab raw this way. Lewis urged him to try a small piece, so he did. We all laughed at the face he made. "I think I like it better cooked." Mother promised to boil the next one she caught. We like it boiled, too.

Now that the ice has formed all around, Dixon and Lewis and Father go out with the rest of the hunters to look for seal.

DECEMBER 6

The hunters are catching many seals. The big boys were not in school this week. They are hunters, too.

Teacher Roger also. Our mothers were busy cutting up the seals. The rest of us helped them after school. Now there is much good food to eat. Much oil and good skins. Everyone is busy.

DECEMBER 13

We are learning many Christmas carols for our big Christmas party. All of us are making decorations for the schoolhouse. Wooko and Vivian are the parents of a new baby boy named Koyakuk. That was the name of Silook's father, who died in Nome this summer. Wooko and Vivian are proud to have a son with such a fine name.

It was a good winter for hunting. There were many seals for the women to cut and skin. The smaller boys watched for the hunters' return. They ran out to help pull in the seals or walrus for the tired hunters. We all carried the meat and hides up from the shore. Father and Mother put much meat away in our section of the ice cave. Twice Lewis and Dixon were allowed to go on short hunts. Roger and the big boys, Nat and Paul especially, were often gone from school. For a while there was no time to stay after school and work on the knitting. We were having a busy time on our island. That is why we don't mind the short, short daylight and the long, long dark night. We are busy, and we think of good meats to eat, and plenty left over to toss to the dogs.

Christmastime is coming, too, and Father Tomas will hold the services in the church. Then the longest day of dark of the whole year will have passed, and soon after we will see the sun for longer and longer until there is only a little bit of dark left to remind us that it is there, waiting to come back again. Yes, we are happy and laughing this season.

At school we sing and sing to prepare for the Christmas program. First we learn to sing "Jingle Bells" and "Silent Night." Etta has written the words of "Silent Night" in the language of our people, and we learn that, too. We girls help Marie make candy while Roger and the boys pop popcorn on top of the stove. After they have popped a dishpan and two bucketfuls, Marie makes some syrup. She colors some of it red and some of it green and pours it on the popcorn to make red and green popcorn balls. We are not allowed to eat any yet. They all must be saved for the night of the program, but we get to eat the bits of popcorn that are left in the pans. We do not want to go home this day after school. It smells too good in the schoolhouse.

Oh, that Christmas was a wonderful time for us. We at school worked and worked so hard to sing our songs just right. We did our lessons as fast as we could so we could knit and finish our socks or mittens. We drew pictures and put them all over the schoolroom. We hung paper chains made by the littlest ones around the windows, and on the blackboard there were pictures. Teachers made a line down the big blackboard, and on one half Roger and Marie and Dixon showed us a Wisconsin Christmas. There was a Christmas tree and a church with snow falling all around it, and there was a house with a Santa Claus and a reindeer up on its top. On the other half of the blackboard Nat drew a King Island Christmas. There was our village, little square wooden houses perched like birds' nests with the drying racks and the oomiaks resting upside down. Father Tomas stood in the door of the church, welcoming the people. Nat is a good artist, and he showed all the people, tiny people, coming up the stairs and pathways, up to the church for Christmas. Teachers said Nat was a real artist. It made us all happy and proud to hear that. It is true that Nat's picture showed up the crookedness and lopsidedness of the Wisconsin side of the blackboard. Roger and Marie and Dixon laughed when Nat was finished.

"Well," Roger said, "you can see that we are teachers and not artists, that's for sure." But we liked the pictures of two such different Christmases, and we looked and looked at the board. This is what I will remember forever, I said to myself. Nat has made King Island look just like it is, and I will always see it here behind my eyes just as Nat made it on the blackboard at the school for Christmas.

EIGHT

Everyone came to the schoolhouse for the program, except Pica, who was so sick again with TB he did not feel like going anywhere. Ruth has TB, too, but she says she is too old and too tough for anything to bother her. Some of our King Islanders have always had TB, and some have spent a long time down in the big hospital and have come home well again. This happened in my father's time before I was born. Pica, too, came home well, but now he is sick again. That is the way it is. Vivian did not come to the program, either, but Wooko was there with Rose and little Olga. Koyakuk was not feeling good, I knew, because our mother had been at Vivian's, helping her.

Everyone liked the singing and the decorations. The red and green popcorn balls made us laugh. Ooloranna looked at his for a long time. He turned it around and around and put out his tongue and tasted it. "Hey," he said, "how can I eat this thing? My teeth are worn down from chewing tough blubber and frozen walrus. Hey, hey, here is a thing for sure!" We all laughed, and many people offered to eat his popcorn ball.

Before the dancing Roger showed a movie. He had saved it especially for the Christmas program. It was short, so he showed it twice, and he promised to show it again, later on. It was about a little boy who could not walk without a crutch and he gave his crutch to the baby Jesus and then he could walk.

Next day we had the biggest church service of the year. There were candles everywhere, and Father Tomas wore his best robes. When it was over, we went to the schoolhouse for the feast. Everyone had brought something good to eat. There was so much I couldn't taste it all. I wanted to be sure I had some of Etta's pickled walrus flipper and some of Barbara's seal liver, and some pork and beans over a slice of Marie's soft bread. There were so many canned peaches we could have as much as we wanted. That's what Father Tomas always brings to the feast. He knows how much we love them. "Let Nat and Paul have an extra helping," he called out. "They carried these peaches up from the shore to the church last fall."

"If you'd told us why that box was so heavy," Paul said, laughing, "we wouldn't have complained so much. We are always ready to work for something so good to eat."

Lewis couldn't wait for the ice cream. We save it for the very last, it is so good. He had been telling Dixon and telling Dixon about it. He had Dixon so curious that he was as eager for it to be served as Lewis. Our mother and Ruth make the best. Mother had carefully saved a big bucket of Nome blueberries just for the ice cream, and Ruth had brought back raw reindeer fat from Nome to use. Mother didn't have any reindeer fat, so she used white shortening from our big can. She says if you beat and beat it as you should, it tastes just as good.

"This is *ice cream?*" asked Dixon, eyeing the big full dishpans that Ruth and Mother placed proudly on the table. Everyone was eager to have a taste, and there was lots of happy laughing and smacking of lips. "What are those black and red things in it?" asked Dixon. He was looking at his plate with a funny expression on his face.

Lewis explained, "The red dots are fish eggs, and the black ones are dried blueberries. Mother takes some fat and beats and beats it with seal oil. Then she puts in the berries and fish eggs and beats it some more. Doesn't it just melt in your mouth?" Lewis was teasing Dixon because Dixon had been telling him about Wisconsin ice cream that melts in the mouth like snow in the sun.

Dixon took a tiny taste while Lewis and I watched. "Not bad," he said. "It's not so bad." We laughed. "It does kinda melt in your mouth all right." He swallowed hard and took another tiny bite. "But it's not sweet. Our ice cream is sweet and cold."

Lewis and I have eaten the real ice cream in Nome. It is good, but our ice cream is better. It has more taste and flavor. Lewis was happy to finish his friend Dixon's ice cream. "Next time you will like it better."

When Ooloranna got out his drum, it was time for the dancing and singing. First the men danced to the drum beating, leaping and swinging their arms. Then the women danced, sitting all in a row and waving their white-gloved hands. Dixon asked me why the women sit to dance. "Oh," I said, "sometimes they do stand up, but they stand with their feet so still anyway that when there is not much room, they can sit just as well." The women's dance is all hand and body movement.

In our village we love it when the drums begin and the dancing starts. Sometimes, the small children get up and join the dancing, at the outer edges, where they are not in the way. Sometimes, too, we older children dance in the clubhouse, imitating the dancing at the parties. If any of the older women are there, they will laugh and join us and tell us how it was done in the old days. "Hey, now," they say approvingly. "That is how it is done."

Now the men are going to have a tug-of-war. Teacher got out the rope, and Adsun and Peter stepped up to be first. They each looped an end of the rope around their necks. They held out their

hands and strained back as hard as they could. How they pulled. Everyone was quiet. Sweat ran in trickles down the faces of the two men. Neither moved across the floor. We could hear their heavy breathing, pant, pant. Then Peter had to move. Adsun moved back with a great heave, and he had won. There was lots of joking and teasing as Tan and Yakuk stepped up to have a try. After them came Wana and Al. Next Adsun challenged Yakuk, who had won, and then he also pulled Wana. Now it was time for Eir to come forward. He has a crippled leg, but for a long time no one has been able to win over Eir in the tug-of-war. Dixon is busy telling Lewis how a tug-of-war is done in his village in Wisconsin. Teacher Roger says he will show the boys how it is done when school starts again and we can have a recess time out on the ice. "That kind of tug-of-war takes a lot of space," he said.

Eir stands with his one crutch, and Adsun pulls, pulls, pulls. But Eir does not move, and finally Adsun has to admit defeat.

Now comes the ear-pulling contest. "Ouch," cried Dixon when he saw how the string was tied to the ears of the opponents. "Doesn't that hurt? Boy, that looks like it would hurt a lot!"

"We men of King Island are strong, and we do not mind a little pain," bragged Lewis. "We are tough."

Pica always has won the ear pull, but now that he is sick, someone else will be the best one. It is Peter. That is big Peter, not George's little Peter, who just started school. No one can budge big Peter even a little bit.

Next comes the thumb wrestle and the finger pull. Our own father is the champion of the thumb wrestle and has been for a long time. Yakuk wins the finger pull. It is followed by another tug-of-war. This time a long, tapered pole is grasped at opposite ends. Each man holds the slick, narrow end of the pole in a tightly clenched fist. Only one hand can be used. It is so hard to hold onto that pole. Adsun is the best at this. When Dixon and Lewis try it, it is easy for Lewis to pull the stick right out of Dixon's hand. "Let's try it again." Dixon cannot understand how it is so easy for Lewis to take that pole away from him when he is so much bigger. But hang on as hard as he can, he cannot win the pole away from Lewis.

"Let me show you how to arm wrestle," Dixon said. So all the boys try wrestling with Dixon. At first he wins, but as soon as the other boys learn how to do it, he is bested every time. "There sure is something about living on King Island that makes you strong, I guess," he said.

Nat and Paul, the two biggest boys in the school, decide to try it. They are the same size and age, and both have always lived on King Island. Everyone stops to watch them. For a long time they strain and push, each trying so hard to force the other's hand down to the table. Paul's arm wavers, but it does not go all the way down, and now he has managed to get it up again and over a bit to Nat's side. Back and forth they go, but neither can put the other's hand down on the table. Everyone is watching. This is some contest! Ooloranna called to them, "Ho, boys, it is easy to see that you are young men of King Island!" Finally Roger declares it is a tie, and they both are winners.

Oh, that was the best Christmas I ever remember.

NINE

On New Year's Day we had another service at the church and another feast at the schoolhouse. Then we all went out into the frosty night with our fireworks. Roger and Dixon had a good box of Roman candles and pinwheels and skyrockets. Father had gotten Lewis and me each a package of sparklers and a package of small firecrackers. We were brighter than the northern lights, the great aurora borealis that goes crackling and whipping across our northern skies when the weather is cold and clear. Almost all the other children had firecrackers and sparklers, too, so we made a great noise and a fine show to welcome in the new year.

Back in the schoolhouse we had hot chocolate and tea, and Ooloranna said what a fine year it had been. "The days of long light are coming, and if we are lucky, many walrus and—who knows?—maybe a polar bear or two will be slain by our hunters. Then, God be willing, some beluga will come our way, and we will be able to give thanks that we have had good food for all this year on our King Island."

School began again. The days of longer and longer light came quickly. Out on the ice Roger and Dixon showed the school how to play baseball. The boys marked the bases on the ice and played baseball whenever they could. Lily and I could play, too, if we wanted to. Sometimes we did, but sometimes we liked to stay in and knit or sew or help Marie in her kitchen.

Pica died, and Vivian's baby was still sick. Right after the funeral service for Pica there had to be another one for little Koyakuk. Everyone tried to help that baby stay alive, our mother and Roger and Marie and Ruth, but he could not. So we had to make another trip to the graveyard above the church, where Koyakuk's little black box rested beside Pica's. The wood and tar paper to make the coffins were stored under the schoolhouse. It is our father who makes the box for the dead and covers it all over with layers of black tar paper. We pile on big rocks so it will be safe from the dogs. In the old days the dead were covered with stones. There are many of these old graves on King Island, but now we bring over lumber and tar paper on the *North Star*. We all are very sad for Vivian and Wooko that their baby died, and many candles are lit in the church.

TEN

Now there is a constant watch for the coming of the walrus. The men take turns standing for hours, eyes and ears alert.

"How can you hear walrus coming?" Dixon asked Lewis. We three had climbed to a narrow ledge above our village where we often play. There we could see Silook standing watch above us on a big rocky ledge with his binoculars, looking out to the sea beyond the ice. Lewis had been telling Dixon how a walrus hunt differed from a seal hunt. To hunt a seal requires great patience and endurance. The hunter must find the spot where the seal comes up in the leads in the ice and shoot it before it can duck away. Walrus herds are first sighted through the binoculars; then the hunters in the boats must locate the herd by sound and surprise them before they can flop off the ice and swim away. A walrus herd is very noisy. You can hear them whoofing and barking many miles across the ice.

"Soon," Lewis told Dixon. "Soon the first walrus will come. We will keep watch all the time now so

we get to spot the very first walrus. Then the hunters will go out."

"Do you think they will let us go with them sometime?" asked Dixon.

"Perhaps," Lewis said. "If there is room in an
oomiak."

"Uncle Roger wants to go, I know."

"He will want you to go, too," Lewis said. "My
father will take me with him some of the time. He
wants me to learn the old ways as well as the new.
He says I will have need of them."

"Will you go?" Dixon asked, turning to me.

Lewis laughed, but he said sternly, "Women do
not go hunting."

"Oh, I know that," Dixon said. "But I thought
maybe everyone should see a walrus hunt since this
is the last year you will be living here. Uncle Roger
says . . ." Dixon stopped.

"There will always be hunting," Lewis cried.
"How else will there be meat to eat and skins to
make oomiaks and boots and fur for the parkas?"

As for me, I did not like to hear the talk of leaving
the island forever, so I turned away from the boys
and went home. As I scrambled down the rocky
path behind the schoolhouse, I could not help think-

ing of their words. How would we survive, we people of King Island? Then behind my eyes came the picture of Dixon and Lewis standing there on the ledge. Dixon was dressed in a fur parka and mukluks Roger had had Alberta and Ruth make for him. Except for his blue eyes and pale pink skin he looked like a King Island boy. Lewis was wearing a blue plaid jacket ordered from Sears while we were in Nome, a jacket just like the ones many of our boys wore when it was not the coldest weather. On his black hair he wore his baseball cap turned sideways.

I knew that there were some of us who did not want to stay in Nome next year. There was much talk of this at the clubhouse and during the evenings at the schoolhouse, where we played games, did our sewing, heard music, or watched a picture show. Ooloranna and Peter said we could not stay without a school and without a store to help us when we ran out of sugar, flour, or tea. But Paul, big Paul, said he thought King Islanders should not go to Nome but should start a new village at Cape Woolley.

"Those shacks our people live in at Nome are not right. They do not keep out the cold, and the sickness there is worse than ever with too many people crowded into those shanties. It will bring TB back worse than before. We're better off here even without the store."

"But we need to be near the hospital and the doctor in Nome, I say," George argued.

"He's right," Silook said. "And what about school? How can we do without a school where our kids can learn something?"

"If we got together again at Cape Woolley, the Bureau of Indian Affairs would have to build us a school there," big Paul went on. "It isn't so far from Nome and the hospital. We can get there easily in our boats as long as the water isn't frozen, and with our sleds and dogs when winter comes. There is plenty of hunting there, and we would be nearer to King Island."

"Yes, yes, what you say is true," agreed Ooloranna. "But how are we going to build new homes without wood, hey?"

"Yes," said Yakuk. "Driftwood is only good for fires, not for building houses."

Big Paul nodded. "We will have to get some help from the government and the Bureau of Indian Affairs. If we get the lumber, we can build the houses ourselves."

"Yes, yes," said Ooloranna. "But the government is so slow. You, me, we'll all be dead and gone before we get one stick of wood for houses. Too much talk, talk, all the time talk." Everyone laughed and nodded. Big Paul said he would go to the meeting in Kotzebue with the Bureau of Indian Affairs and see if he could get help. Ooloranna agreed that he should go. "You go," he said. "Too much talk-talk for an old man like me. But first we'll go to Nome and stay and let the children go to school, hey."

"Not me," said Silook.

"Not me neither," said Adsun. "I will return next fall as always."

When I first heard that Silook and Adsun and their families were going to return to King Island next year, I was so glad. Maybe our father would decide to do that, too. How would it be, I wondered, if so few of us came back? What would it be like during the ice and the long dark not to have the father in church to hold services and no Christmas and Easter with candles? Could we do without the school with its long row of windows looking out on the clouds of snow sweeping in from the ocean? Could we do without the school to have the meetings and the feasts and the dances and the games?

Would there be enough hunters to find the seals and walrus to keep us all in meat and to put some by in the ice cave for the times when the hunters came home with nothing but cold and empty hands? Adsun and Silook have only big children who are no longer in school, but Silook's son and daughter-in-law will have a baby, and will there be a midwife to help them with the birthing? And who would give us first aid, and where would we keep the lumber and tar paper for the coffins if the schoolhouse were not open?

I could not turn away from the talk because it was everywhere. I did not bother to ask our father if we would be one of the families to return with Adsun and Silook. I already knew what his answer would be. He had told us too many times about his stay in the hospital and how he had learned there how important it was for the future that we learn other ways in the days to come. He would be glad of one thing, I knew. In Nome there was a school, and Lewis and I could go on to high school. Why, some of our people had even gone to the university. Willie Ipalook became a doctor.

ELEVEN

I wrote in the school log every Friday as Marie asked me to.

FEBRUARY 7

A big day this week. The U.S. Navy icebreaker Burton Island arrived. Everyone on King Island watched the big ship ram into the ice to get closer to shore. The Burton Island comes every year. We dress up, greet her, trade our ivory carvings for candy and cigarettes. The Burton Island has a doctor and dentist. Teachers lined up everybody to be examined.

We all were invited to see the big movie about cowboys. Then the men on the ship passed out cake and bananas, apples, and oranges. Everyone got some before the ship left. Big day.

FEBRUARY 14

Everyone has a cold. We all are sneezing and coughing. It is always so after the Burton Island's visit. Teacher explained to us about germs, but not everyone believed her. Ruth was the sickest. She said a bad spirit got her, but she was too tough for it. She feels better now.

FEBRUARY 28

The longer days come fast now. There are many walrus, more than in the last few years. Everyone is happy about that. There was very bright sun for many days. All the school has been sliding on our sleds. We start behind the schoolhouse and go clear down to the shore ice, under the house, around the oomiak. We go fast, fast.

MARCH 6

Teachers showed slides on toothbrushing. A toothbrush danced up and down over teeth all by itself. It made us laugh. Everyone got a new toothbrush. Everyone wanted a red one. Bits of the red handle make the best lures for bullhead fishing. It stormed for three days this week.

MARCH 27

Everyone wonders if the whales will come soon. No hunter has seen a polar bear this year. Teacher Roger wants very much to hunt polar bear. Silook says there are fewer polar bears every year now. Nat drew

pictures of a walrus hunt on the blackboard. He drew hunters all in a line with their guns pointed at a walrus on a big ice cake.

TWELVE

Peter broke his glasses. Peter has the store at his house, and he told everyone who came that he was going to call on the radio for a mail drop to have some new glasses sent out from Nome, and he would take orders from anyone who wanted anything for the pilot to bring out. He, Peter, would collect the money to pay the pilot and the store for all the things ordered. Many people wanted things. Our mother wanted a new teakettle. The men with money wanted cigarettes. Wooko wanted a bottle of whiskey, but Peter said no whiskey, so Vivian paid the money and said "raisins." The store has not had any raisins since Christmas. Roger said if there was going to be a drop, he needed some more medicine, and he gave Peter a list. Over in Nome, Jack Bauer, the pilot, would collect all the items Peter had asked for by radio. He would also stop at the post office and bring any mail for King Island and take mail back.

Jack said he would try to land his small plane on our shore ice on Tuesday at about noon. The men found the smoothest ice, and everyone in school worked to make it smoother for the little plane to set down on. We marked the area off with empty oil drums from the church and school and watched the weather anxiously. Everyone wanted to get some mail. Tuesday was a bright, clear day, and we were glad, but Teacher said there might be too much wind.

When we heard the plane, we all rushed down to the shore. For a time Jack flew the little plane back and forth, inspecting the landing strip we had made. But he did not come down. Roger and Peter went back to the schoolhouse to talk to Jack on the radio.

"Too bad," Peter said when they returned. "Jack says the downdrafts are too strong. He can't land, but he will try to drop everything."

We watched eagerly as Jack flew over us several times, testing the wind. Then, while he flew as low as he could, the plane door opened, and boxes and bags came tumbling out. They were strewn all over the ice. The plane went so fast that some of the things fell so far away we couldn't see where they landed.

We hurried out to pick up things before they were blown away. The boxes had burst, and there were packages and sacks everywhere. We carried things up to the schoolhouse, where Roger and Peter had the lists. Poor Peter, his new glasses were smashed worse than the old ones.

It took the rest of the daylight to find some of the packages. They had scattered for miles. The boys thought it was great fun to go searching over the ice.

"Jack will have to wait for his money until summer," said Peter, tucking the money he had collected into an envelope. He gave back the letters people had written. "You can hand them to your relatives when you see them next summer." He sighed. "What am I going to do with two pairs of broken glasses?"

We all got some letters from relatives in Nome and Teller and Wales. We got a letter from our uncle Ronald, who wrote that the seal hunting had been very bad in Teller. He himself had caught only three seals. That made us feel lucky that seals had been so plentiful around us this winter.

Teachers got the new catalogs, and everyone went to the schoolhouse in the evenings to look at them. The catalogs got a lot of use in the next few weeks, I can tell you.

We don't know how much of that drop from Jack Bauer was lost, but we think not much. Teacher said he sure was glad he got his medicines because after the mail came, we all had another round of colds.

"How come these colds come with the mail?" Peter wanted to know. Teacher was giving him some aspirin for his fever.

"I guess the germs come over on the packages we ordered from Nome," said Roger.

"I didn't see anything, only my broken glasses and the papers and letters and cans and things."

"I've explained, Peter, that germs are so small they can be seen only under a strong magnifying glass. It's these tiny germs that give us the colds. And once one person has a cold, he gives it to another and so on."

Peter said, "Oh, yes, I've been told that before." He took his aspirin and went home, but the look on his face said: tell me another. Roger has shown us more than once a movie that has germs flying through the air and sticking to unwashed hands. We all have seen it, but our people mostly don't believe it.

"Yes, oh, yes." Ruth nodded when she saw it. "The doctors tell me that I have TB because of those little things no one can see. I don't see how things I can't see can make me have a fever and a cough." But Father Tomas says it is true, so it must be so.

Ruth and Ooloranna were very sick with this second cold, and we in the village were worried about them. They are the oldest couple on our island, and Ooloranna is our chief. Vivian and our mother took them food, and Roger and Marie took them medicines. We were glad when they got better and came back to the schoolhouse in the evenings. Dixon had everyone playing checkers; he started a tournament for anyone who wanted to play. He taught all the boys; most of the men already knew how to play. Dixon says we King Islanders are hard to beat at checkers. So far our father, Matthew Atoolik, is at the top of the checkers ladder, but Ooloranna says he may take a game and then, look out, hey, he will be the champion. He says he played checkers a lot when he was young.

Etta is the winner among the women and girls.

She also teases our father, threatening to play him and win. So far they only make fun and have not played. Maybe one day they will, though.

THIRTEEN

Now is the very best time of all on King Island. The hunters expect the whales to start coming north, and the storms don't last, and the sun shines for long, long hours and melts the snow that is frozen onto the rock. We on this island do not get whale very often. Father explained to Dixon that our island is too far out from the mainland to see more than a stray whale or two. It is a great prize when our hunters bring one in. Like polar bear, it is a rare but wonderful thing. The shore ice is still firm, and our mother can still catch crab through the ice, but soon it will be breaking up and the birds will come flying back to make their nests. How we long for fresh eggs and auklet in the pot!

Maybe after Easter the hunters will bring in a

whale. There is plenty of seal and walrus meat in the village ice cave, but there is no whale left, and no one has tasted muktuk for a long time. Dixon, of course, asked Lewis to tell him what muktuk is and what it tastes like. "It is something whales give to us Eskimos." Lewis cannot help teasing Dixon. "You won't like it. *Gussuks* never like it. It's the skin of a whale with the fat, blubber you call it, and it keeps the whale warm when he swims in the cold water, and he gives it to us Eskimos to eat so we can keep warm, too. An Eskimo who eats plenty of blubber can sit by a seal hole all day long and not feel the cold," boasted Lewis.

Nighttime is the best time to catch birds and gather eggs. It does not get too dark to see all night long now, and the birds are quiet in their nests. We are glad to see the birds returning. Some stay and build their nests and lay their eggs; some only rest awhile before flying on north.

Father said that this was the night that we would go to hunt for birds and eggs.

"Dixon wants to go with us," Lewis said. "I'll go tell him to be ready when the sun sets."

Father nodded his permission. "Perhaps Marie and Roger will want to come, too."

"Vivian and her girls are coming with us," Mother said. "Wooko is out with Adsun and Ooloranna, hoping for a whale." We were happy to have company, and we all know how to be quiet enough to catch the birds. Roger and Marie went with us last year.

Father brought his bird nets. He did not want to waste any shot on birds. Lewis was going to show Dixon how to catch an auklet with a noose. "You have to be quiet and then move quickly to catch an auklet." Roger had some nets, too, and Marie brought a big basket for the eggs.

We climbed up the steep cliffs of our rocky island. That is where the birds like to build their nests. This is something I love to do—to climb over the rocks, looking for nests. If we put the eggs in the ice cave, they will keep for a long time. So we want to gather as many as we can. But we do not take all the eggs from any one nest. We always leave some so there will be plenty of young birds for next year. Mother and Marie and I stayed together, but each of us found many different nests. Rose and Olga stayed close to Vivian and helped her carry back her eggs. Startled birds flew up, squawking and crying, then settled back on their nests as soon as we moved on.

There was a north wind blowing, but it was not a strong or stormy wind, and we did not mind its sharpness. We were too busy with our harvest.

We sat down to rest in a sheltered spot, and Marie poured hot, sweet tea for us from her thermos. Mother pulled pilot biscuits from her parka pocket, and we dipped them into our tea. Vivian said she was ready to go home. Rose and Olga were getting sleepy, and probably Wooko would have returned by now. Mother and Marie and I stayed with the hunters until the sun was nearly ready to rise. We had plenty of eggs.

The men and boys came loaded with auklets. We scrambled down the cliffs, sleepy but happy with our night's hunting. Across from the schoolhouse we left some birds and eggs for Father Tomas to find when he got up. Marie gave Mother many of her eggs, too, saying she could not use them all. They still had so much of the powdered eggs left. We know they do not like the eggs as much as we do. I can imagine what a face Dixon will make when he tastes auklet eggs for the very first time! He was happy because he managed to snare two birds. "It was hard to be quick enough. Worse than trying to catch a lizard," he said. Then he tried to explain to

Lewis what a lizard was and how it can leave its tail right in your hand and slide away. Roger said he thought he could find a picture of a lizard to show Lewis, and I thought I would be there so he could show it to me, too.

FOURTEEN

The long light has come. The shore ice begins to break up now. It drifts away in chunks of all sizes. The hunters can no longer go out on the ice but must guide their smallest oomiaks through the leads between ice floes. If they climb up to wait for seal or walrus, they must be very careful that a chunk does not break off and carry them away, away from their boat and far out to sea. Sometimes hunters are lost this way. But our men on King Island choose their hunting spots only after they have looked and looked to make sure it is safe. The shore ice will soon be gone entirely, and there will be no more baseball or soccer. Our playing field will have melted away.

Etta and Marie and Roger are busy packing up all the things in the school, and so is Father Tomas in the church. They say they just don't know how everything is going to fit into the oomiaks for the trip to Nome. The six biggest boats will make the trip and will have to carry everyone. Since we are not coming back in the fall, there is so much more to take. I am worried about our two dogs. Will there be room for them to go to Nome with us?

Silook and Adsun still say they are returning, and Vivian tries very hard to get Wooko to say he will return; she told my mother that it would be better for Rose and Olga to miss school than for Wooko to be in Nome and drink up all their money. But Wooko refuses. Adsun talked and talked to Ooloranna. He knows if our chief says so, more will join him in returning. "I do not want to leave our home either," Ooloranna said. "But Ruth has TB, and she must be nearer the doctor and the hospital. Her cough is not getting better here on the island." Ruth says she does not need medicine, but she does not say she wants to return to the island for another winter either.

Big Paul does not want Adsun and Silook to return. He says that if every King Islander backs him and agrees to Cape Woolley, he will have a good chance to get the Bureau of Indian Affairs to help us start a new village there, and we can be together again. "There will be only seventeen of you to come back," he says to Silook and Adsun. "You know what that means. With no church and no teachers at the school you will find you don't want to be here alone another year or two." There was much talk in the schoolhouse, in the clubhouse, everywhere. It made my heart very heavy to hear it. Father said to Mother that big Paul was right, that we all should go one way and show everyone we are King Islanders. But Silook and Adsun insisted they were going to return, and their families with them. I think my father is right, but I wish very much that I, too, could return on the big *North Star* and see our big rock rising steep and sheer out of the sea and hear the dogs barking on the shore, glad to see us coming home after our summer away.

FIFTEEN

There was much to write in the log-book the last Friday of school. We had a last-day program, and the best thing was that the day before, our father and Silook and Peter and Yakuk and big Paul brought in a beluga whale and we had what we like so much and what we had not had a taste of for so long. At the party for the last day of school there was beluga stew! Dixon finally got to taste muktuk, and he said he really liked it but he liked it best boiled. We like it both ways, raw or cooked. That whale made a lot of excitement! This year we have had no polar bear at all, and the men say that whales and polar bears are getting harder and harder to find, also seals and walrus in some places.

The dogs got in another big fight they were so excited. But there was whale meat to throw to them. That stopped them. They would rather eat than fight. The sun shone so long that day, and everyone was happy.

There are just a few feet of shore ice left. June has come, and the very longest day of the year is near.

The next storm that sweeps in across the sea will break up the last of the ice, and it will be time to go. There will be no more walrus when the ice is gone, and it will be time to sell the ivory carvings in Nome.

Marie came by our house to see if Mother and I would climb up to the top of King Island with her. "I just want to have one last look," she said. Lily was there, so she came, too. Up, up we climbed, up past the schoolhouse and the church, up past the graveyard, where the two newest additions, Pica and little Koyakuk, lay side by side. The tar paper was weathered and bleached, but they were still safe, and Father Tomas has said their spirits have gone to our Father in heaven.

The top of King Island is flat, flat. There the wind is always blowing. From there you can see the sea in all directions. We see that the ice is nearly gone. And in the north we see a big bank of black and heavy clouds.

"Storm coming," Mother said. "Big one."

Marie nodded. "Yes, I see it. This means we will leave, doesn't it?"

"Yes," Mother said.

"Well, I'm as nearly packed as I'll ever be. I just

hope we aren't trying to carry too much."

We hurried down to be home before the wind and rain. The waves were smashing the rest of the ice away, and word went around the village: "Time to leave, time to go, be ready when the storm dies."

So those were our last three days on King Island. It is ninety miles across the open ocean to Nome, and with the outboard motors working as hard as they can, it will take us all of a long day to get there. We must leave just when the storm is over so that the seas will be calm and smooth for us the whole way. Yakuk climbs up where he can look out toward the mainland and see just the moment when the storm is safely over. Yakuk of the sharp eyes will watch and watch for us all. He will tell us when he sees the storm is coming to an end. Then we will hurry, hurry and pile everything into the boats as fast as we can.

SIXTEEN

Toward evening of the third day Yakuk brought the word to start loading. Teacher says it is the fifteenth of June.

Everyone carries big loads down to the shore. The piles grow bigger and bigger. So much has to go. There is even some of the blubber left to take. The muktuk of the white beluga is the very best in all the world, so we always try to make it last a long while.

Each oomiak has a captain, and he sees to the loading of his boat. Father is one. We are taking the teachers and Dixon, Wooko and Vivian, Rose and Olga, Peter and Barbara and Etta Penetac, Annie and John Kokulerk, Theresa Omiak and Simon Pushruk, Tan, and Eir and his wife, Alice Pikougona.

We pass the piles beside our oomiak into the boat as fast as we can, everyone helping. Is there going to be any room left for us to squeeze into? The dogs know we are going, and they are whining and barking among the rocks on the shore and getting in the way.

When we all are in, Father and Simon and Tan fasten paddles up along the sides of the boat, and canvas is strung up to keep the waves from splashing in and swamping us. The sides of our oomiak are close to the water, oh, so close, because we are carrying so much and so many. We have done this many times before, and the men know just how much each oomiak can carry, but we know we are stretching it this year.

Ooloranna stands up and gives the signal to leave. Quick as a flash our father tosses in our two dogs. Lewis smiles, and I, too, give a big grin. Now Tan has his dog, so we have three dogs going to Nome in our oomiak.

Father starts the outboard. The others are starting now, too, and the dogs left onshore know what that means. What mournful howls rise up from their throats. So much noise makes all the birds start up, screeching and crying. As we chug away, the sky over King Island is black with them, calling and crying to us. Like the dogs, I think, they say: Come back, come back. But we head out to sea, and it is only moments before we round the point and our village can be seen no more. The barking of the dogs and the cries of the birds can no longer be heard,

only the steady chug-chug of our motor and the slap of the waves hitting against the walrus hide of our boat.

There is a fresh wind blowing, and in spite of the sun which has come out of the clouds to make a bright clear evening, it is cold. I snuggle down in my parka and feel glad about our dogs.

Vivian has started to cry. She does not want to go to Nome, where Wooko will go to the bars and drink up their money. She cries and says that she does not want to leave her son there alone on King Island even if his spirit has gone to heaven. She cries and moans quietly to herself. She does not have Mary on the shore to look forward to as I do. She is not glad about the school there for her children as our father and mother are for me and Lewis. She thinks that the hospital and the doctor were too far away to save her little Koyakuk, so what good are they to her now? She cries and cries.

I, too, am sad in spite of the good things I can see ahead. I do not want to go and never come back again. I want to see my home again as I have always done, every year, sure as sure. Behind my eyes I see our village just as Nat drew it on the blackboard, our tiny village perched on our steep, steep rock with all the steps and trails winding up and under and around to my house and the school and church. Inside myself I cry, too, as I say goodbye to my King Island. I know that in my heart there will be tears forever.

AFTERWORD

The closing of the King Island school in 1964 marked the end of a way of life for the islanders. For a year or two longer a few did return to the island for the winter, but gradually the abandoned World War II huts in Nome in which they had camped summers became their permanent home.

The story is not a happy one. In ten years these buildings became miserable slums. The damp and crowded living quarters fostered the return of tuberculosis, which had been wiped out by a vigorous decade of health services and preventive care during the fifties. There was little work, and few of the islanders had good jobs. Although officials were sympathetic to their plight, and Paul Tiulana, a native leader, made repeated efforts to establish a new home for his people at Cape Woolley, his plan was never realized.

It was not until 1974, when the Bering Sea flooded the coastal areas of northeastern Alaska and the shacks were totally demolished, that the Bureau of Indian Affairs stepped in. New houses were built on the east side of town, safely out of reach of even the angriest waters. Some of the elders moved to Anchorage, where the large Alaska Native Hospital could give them the medical treatment they needed.

The economic plight of the King Islanders is not easily solved. Carving ivory remains a source of income, and many King Islanders spend their summers at Cape Woolley, where they have established a fishing camp. They also go back to their beloved island to hunt walrus and seal and join other Eskimos in the annual Nome area reindeer roundup each spring. They vaccinate and treat the herds and collect antlers for sale to Korea and China.

In 1971 the Indians and Eskimos of Alaska had settled a massive land claim with the U.S. government. Some small amounts of money were distributed individually, but most of it was used to set up native corporations to invest and handle the settlement. King Islanders belong to the Bering Straits Corporation. Within it they have remained a tightly knit group, the King Island Village Corporation, proud of their heritage and determined to let their young people know their background and history and to preserve important parts of their culture.

Television, which now brings the latest in general entertainment to even the most remote Alaskan village, has created new problems. Elders complain that young people are no longer interested in learning the old ways. But they have not given up. In 1982, at the Bering Straits Elders Conference, King Islanders revived the historic wolf dance. It was the first performance of this ancient ritual in some fifty years. The event was much publicized, and videotapes of this and other cultural events are helping keep the history and customs of the King Islanders alive.

JEAN ROGERS was born in Wendell, Idaho, and holds a B.A. degree from the University of California, Berkeley. She now lives in Juneau, Alaska, with her husband. They have six adopted children, Geoffrey, Gavin, and Garth and Shelley, Sidney, and Sabrina (only one of whom is still at home).

She is the recipient of an Honored Author citation from the Alaska State Reading Association. *Goodbye, My Island* is her first book for children.

RIE MUÑOZ was born in Los Angeles and studied art at Washington and Lee University and the University of Alaska. She has lived in Alaska since 1950 and spent the year from 1951 to 1952 as a teacher in the King Island of this story. It is on her experience there that *Goodbye, My Island* is based.

Today she is an honored artist, whose work is represented in the permanent collections of the Alaska State Museum in Juneau, the Anchorage Historical and Fine Arts Museum, as well as in many private collections. Her home is in Juneau.